TOOTHE

Tooth Fairy in Training

by
Kristin Neva

Illustrated by
Josiah Mleko

Toothella — Tooth Fairy in Training

Copyright © 2018 by Kristin Neva

Illustrations by Josiah Mleko

Published by
The Christmas Tree House
Hancock, MI 49930 U.S.A.

ISBN 978-0-9981962-6-8

KristinNeva.com

THE
CHRISTMAS TREE
HOUSE

"Wake up!" said Abby, as she shook Mom's shoulder.

"Are you okay? What's wrong?" asked Mom.

"The tooth fairy didn't come!" Abby sobbed.

"She didn't?!" Mom sat up.

"Why didn't she take my tooth?" asked Abby.

"Something must have happened," said Mom, putting her arm around Abby's shoulder.

Abby thought. "I bet I got a tooth fairy in training."

"Toothella!" called Fairy Mom. She flew into the room.
"What's taking you so long?"

"Just a minute." Toothella read quickly.

"I will take that book, and you will have no *Pretty Pink Princess* for a week if you don't get a move on," said Mom.

Toothella looked up. "But I need to find out if she escapes."

"You'll have to find out later," said Mom. "You need to get ready!"

Toothella put the book down and pulled a skirt over her leotard.

"You have a busy night tonight," said Mom. "There are seven teeth to collect, so you must hurry. The children will be awake soon."

"I can do it," said Toothella. She twisted a scrunchie around her ponytail.

"I'm a fast flier." Toothella zoomed to the ceiling. "See?"

"I know you are," said Mom. "You just have a habit of getting distracted."

"You mean like the time I took a little nap in Claire's dollhouse?" asked Toothella.

"Yes," said Mom.

"Or the time I went for a ride on Isaac's train?" asked Toothella.

"Exactly," said Mom. "Tonight you need to stay focused. No distractions. In and out! Now come down and finish getting ready."

Toothella flew down and put on her pink slippers. "It won't take me long," she said. "I'll be back before dawn."

"Don't forget your pouch," said Mom.

Toothella strapped the pouch on.

"Here's the list and a map," said Mom.

"Be careful and stay away from night-lights so the children don't see you. Remember, what is seen is not imagined."

"I know," said Toothella. "You say that every night."

Mom hugged Toothella.

Toothella flew out of the forest and into town. First stop — Claire's house.

"In and out," she told herself.

She grabbed a pinch of fairy dust from her pouch and threw it at Claire's window. The glass dissolved, with an opening just big enough for Toothella to dart through. The glass reappeared behind her.

Toothella looked longingly at the
new kitchen in Claire's dollhouse.

"In and out!" she told herself again.

Toothella poked her head under Claire's pillow and found a shiny white tooth. She opened her pouch and took out two coins.

Claire exhaled. Her breath fluttered Toothella's wings.

Toothella left the money and put the tooth in her pouch.

She glanced at Claire's dollhouse as she flew to the window. *In and out. In and out.* With a pinch of fairy dust, she flew through the window and away to the next house.

Toothella did not climb the block tower in Zach's room. "In and out," she told herself.

She did not sit on Isabella's toy horse, even though it was just her size and looked real.

"Maybe next time," she whispered.

Toothella *did* ride in Michael's race car—
but only for a few minutes.

She slid down Anna's slide—but just once.

Well, maybe twice.

Cora's night-light shone stars around the room. Toothella landed in pink light on the dresser. She looked at herself in the mirror and smiled. She was pink. She danced and twirled.

By the time she got to Abby's room, the sun was rising.

Toothella longed to jump on Abby's trampoline, but there was no time. She would have to work fast.

She flew to Abby's bed.

As she opened her pouch, she heard Abby stir.

Toothella darted behind the curtain.

Abby stretched her arms and sat up. She looked under her pillow, took her tooth, and ran from the room.

"Wake up!" Abby yelled from down the hall. "The tooth fairy didn't come."

Toothella sighed.

With the last of her fairy dust, she flew out the window and home to the forest.

She told her mom what had happened.

"Oh, Toothella." Mom gave her a hug. "What am I going to do with you?"

Toothella cried.

"At least you hid quickly so you didn't ruin Abby's imagination," said Mom. "I'll add her to your list for tonight. You can try again."

Toothella clapped her hands. "Abby has a trampoline in her bedroom!"

Made in the USA
Columbia, SC
31 March 2019